NEWMARKET PUBLIC LIBRARY

W9-AMV-678

DATE DUE

COPY 1   1878

J
398   Beauty and the beast.
.209   Beauty and the beast / Mme. Leprince de Beaumont
44   & Binette Schroeder ; retold from the French by Anne
Beaut   Carter ; [illustrations by Binette Schroeder]. -- 1st
            American ed. -- New York : C.N. Potter : Distributed
            by Crown Publishers, 1986.
                36 p. : col. ill. ; 27 cm.

            Based on: Belle et la bête / Madame Leprince de
            Beaumont.
            0267209X   LC: 85028125   ISBN: 0517561735 : J

            1. Fairy tales. – France. I. Leprince de Beaumont,
                                            (See next card)

       2245 LSCB   36JUL30 39   1-67002868
       PRODUCED IN CANADA BY UTLAS Inc.   PRODUIT AU CANADA PAR UTLAS Inc.

Text copyright © 1986 by Anne Carter
Illustrations copyright © 1986 by Binette Schroeder

All rights reserved. No part of this book may be reproduced
or transmitted in any form or by any means, electronic or
mechanical, including photocopying, recording, or by any
information storage and retrieval system, without permission
in writing from the publisher.

Published in the United States of America in 1986 by
Clarkson N. Potter, Inc., 225 Park Avenue South,
New York, New York 10003

First published in Great Britain by Walker Books Ltd.,
184-192 Drummond Street, London NW1 3HP

CLARKSON N. POTTER, POTTER, and colophon are trademarks of
Clarkson N. Potter, Inc.

Manufactured in Italy

Library of Congress Cataloging-in-Publication Data
Carter, Anne.
  Beauty and the beast.
  Based on: *Belle et la bête*/Madame Leprince de
Beaumont.
  Summary: Through her great capacity to love, a
kind and beautiful maid releases a handsome prince
from the spell that has made him an ugly beast.
  [1. Fairy tales. 2. Folklore—France]
  I. Schroeder, Binette, ill. II. Leprince de
Beaumont, Madame (Jeanne-Marie), 1711–1780.
Belle et la bête. III. Title.
PZ8.C2398Be 1986 398.2'0944 [E] 85-28125
ISBN 0-517-56173-5

10 9 8 7 6 5 4 3 2 1
First American Edition

AUG 2 6 1986

FOR BEATRIZ

Mme Le Prince de Beaumont 1711–1780
The Author of "Beauty and the Beast"

BEAUTY

AND THE

BEAST

Mme. LEPRINCE DE BEAUMONT
& BINETTE SCHROEDER

RETOLD FROM THE FRENCH BY ANNE CARTER

CLARKSON N. POTTER, INC./PUBLISHERS
DISTRIBUTED BY CROWN PUBLISHERS, INC./NEW YORK

Once upon a time there was a merchant. He had six children, three girls and three boys and, because he was immensely rich as well as sensible, he had them all given the best education possible.

All of his daughters were beautiful, but the youngest was the loveliest of all. When she was little everyone called her Beauty, and somehow that name clung to her, which made her sisters very jealous. What is more, Beauty was not only better looking than her sisters, she was better in every way. Being so rich had made the two eldest girls very proud. They thought themselves great ladies and were far too grand to make friends with other merchants' daughters. They were always going to balls and plays and showing off in fashionable society and they scoffed at their younger sister for spending all her time at home reading books.

Everyone knew that the girls were amazingly rich, and more than one wealthy merchant came to ask for their hands in marriage. But the two eldest answered that they had no mind to marry, unless it might be to a duke or an earl at least. Beauty thanked all her suitors very kindly but said she was too young and wished to stay with her father for a few years yet.

Then, quite suddenly, the merchant's ships were wrecked at sea, and all his money was lost. Nothing was left to him but one small house in the country. He wept as he told his children that they would have to go there and make a living by working like the peasants.

His two eldest daughters said at once that they had no intention of living anywhere but in the city and that they had young men who would be only too glad to marry them, money or no money.

But in this they were mistaken. Their admirers would not look at them now that they were poor. They were so proud that nobody liked them and people said: 'They don't deserve our pity! We're glad to see them humbled. Let them practice their airs and graces on the sheep!'

At the same time, everyone was sorry for Beauty because she was so sweet and gentle and had always been kind to the poor. There were quite a few gentlemen who would have married her, even without a penny to her name. But she told them she could never bring herself to leave her poor father and meant to go with him to the country to comfort him and help him in his trouble.

When they were settled in their new home, the merchant and his sons set to work farming the land. Beauty learned to get up at four in the morning to keep the house clean and cook dinner for the whole family. She found it hard at first, for she was not used to the life of a maid of all work, but after a month or two she grew stronger and the work only made her pleasantly tired. When it was done, she would read or play her lute or sit singing to herself while she sewed.

Her two sisters, on the other hand, were bored to tears. They lay in bed until ten and spent the remainder of the day bewailing their lost friends and their fine clothes.

'Just look at that stupid sister of ours,' they would say. 'The little idiot actually enjoys this terrible life.'

But the good merchant thought differently. He knew that Beauty was more fit than her sisters to shine in the world and he was full of admiration for her patience and good temper. He could see that her sisters, not content with letting her do all the work of the house, were also as rude to her as they knew how to be.

The merchant and his family had been living in this lonely farmhouse for a year when a letter arrived, saying that one ship, which had been given up for lost, had come safely to port. They were all very excited, but the two eldest daughters were especially pleased because they thought it meant a return to their old way of life. They even helped their father pack his bag and saddle his horse, all the time begging him to bring them expensive presents. Beauty said nothing. It seemed to her that her sisters had already spent all the money their father was likely to gain.

It was not until he was almost ready to ride away that the merchant turned to his youngest daughter.

'Well, Beauty,' he said, smiling at her. 'Your sisters have given me their orders. What would you have?'

Beauty knew she must ask for something if she did not want to hurt his feelings, so she said quickly: 'Thank you, Father. Will you bring me a rose? We have none hereabouts.'

The merchant rode away, full of hope. But when he came to his ship, he found that he had to go to court for his money, so that in the end there was very little profit from the voyage. He turned homewards, tired and depressed, and very nearly as poor as when he had set out.

The weather turned dark and cold. Night was coming but the merchant pressed on, eager to see his home and children again. He had only thirty miles to go. The road led through a deep forest and soon, as the wind rose and snow began to fall, he knew that he was lost.

The trees closed in on either side and he could hear wolves howling in the distance. Whirling snowflakes clogged his mouth and eyelids and twice his horse stumbled and threw him, so that at last he plodded forward on foot, clinging to the reins.

He was sure that he was going to die of cold and exhaustion when suddenly the wind dropped and he saw an opening in the wood and a light twinkling far away in the distance. Turning towards it he found himself in a great avenue of trees. The snow had ceased and the night was very still. The merchant struggled on through the drifts until he could see that the lights came from a huge, glittering castle. He hastened towards it, thanking heaven for his deliverance. But as he passed through the gatehouse, he was surprised to find the courtyard quite empty. Lights were everywhere, but not a groom or a human being of any kind could he see.

The stable doors stood open and his horse, as tired and hungry as himself, at once scented the warm straw and made its own way to the waiting stall. The merchant followed as if in a dream and saw the animal fed and watered before he himself entered the house. In the great hall lights blazed everywhere and a good fire burned on the hearth, but all was as silent and deserted as outside. A table set for one stood near the fire, with food and wine upon it, as though waiting for a guest.

The merchant went towards it, steam rising from his wet clothes. After a moment, feeling that the master of the house, whoever he was, could not begrudge him a little comfort on this stormy night, he helped himself to a glass of wine. Then he took a seat by the fire and dozed until a clock, striking eleven, startled him awake. The sight of the loaded table before him was too much. He could not stop himself. Beginning with a leg of chicken, he ate ravenously and then, as no one had yet appeared, he set out to explore the castle. Each of the rooms he passed through seemed grander than the last until, coming on one that had a good bed in it, he tumbled into it and instantly fell fast asleep.

It was ten in the morning when he woke. To his great surprise he found that his old, travel-worn garments had vanished and in their place was a handsome suit of clothes, like those he had worn in the days when he was rich. He put them on, convinced that the castle must belong to some good fairy who was taking care of him. When he looked out of the window he saw that last night's snow was all gone and a garden full of flowers met his eyes. In the great hall, where he had eaten the previous night, a small table was laid for breakfast and this time the merchant sat down to it with no qualms, thanking the good fairy aloud as he did so.

When he had drunk his chocolate, he went to find his horse. A rose bush, covered with flowers, reminded him of Beauty and of his promise to her.

Smiling, the merchant drew the knife from his belt, seized hold of one flowering branch and cut it off.

At once he heard a dreadful cry. He looked up and beheld, advancing on him, a monstrous beast, so hideous that the merchant nearly fainted with horror.

'Ungrateful man!' The beast spoke in a voice that struck terror into his heart. 'I saved your life by taking you into my castle and this is how you repay me! By stealing my roses which mean more to me than all the world! For that you must pay with your life. You have fifteen minutes to make your peace with God!'

The merchant flung himself on his knees before the beast.

'Oh, my lord, forgive me! I meant no harm. I took the roses for my daughter, because she longed for them.'

'I am not your lord,' the monster growled. 'I am the Beast. Do not try to flatter me. Say what you think. I'll like you better for it. You say you have a daughter?'

'Three, sir.'

'Then I will spare your life, but on condition that one of them is willing to come here and die for you. No! No argument! Only, if your daughters will not give their lives, swear to me that you will return yourself before three months have passed.'

Three months of life seemed to the poor merchant better than none. At least he would have time to say goodbye to his children. For of course he had no intention of allowing any of them to die for him. So he gave his word to the Beast.

'Go then,' the Beast said. 'And because I would not have you leave empty-handed, return first to the room you slept in and fill the chest which you will find there with whatever takes your fancy. I will see that it is carried to your home.'

With that the Beast turned away and the merchant, comforting himself that at least he would not leave his family destitute, did as he was told.

Besides the chest the Beast had mentioned, he found great amounts of gold and jewels in his room. He filled the chest and closed the lid. Then he went thankfully to the stable, saddled his horse and rode out of the castle, a sadder man than he had entered it.

He never knew how long it took him to reach home. His horse seemed to find the way of its own accord. But as his family gathered round him, full of eager welcome, he could not help the tears springing to his eyes as he looked at them. He was still holding the roses he had brought for Beauty and now he gave them to her, saying: 'Take them, Beauty. These roses have cost your poor father very dear.'

His children stared at him in horror as he told them his sad tale. Then the two eldest girls broke out into such shrieks and cries that they seemed half mad. Both of them turned on Beauty and blamed her bitterly for what had happened.

'It's all your fault,' they told her. 'You couldn't be like us! You had to ask for something different! You have brought this trouble on our father. And now you can't even shed a tear for him!'

It was true that Beauty was not crying. But she was standing close by her father and holding his hand in a way that gave him more comfort than all her sisters' clamor.

Now she answered them firmly: 'Why should I weep for him? My father is not going to die. Since the Beast is willing to take one of us in his place, I shall go. The fault, as you say, is all mine.'

At this Beauty's three brothers cried out angrily that she should not sacrifice herself. They would go and slay the Beast.

Their father told them roundly that they were talking nonsense. 'I have seen the power of the Beast,' he said. 'It is so great, we have no hope of destroying him. I am grateful, my dear Beauty,' he added fondly, 'but what kind of father should I be if I were to let you face death for my sake? I am old. My only sorrow will be in losing you, my children.'

'I may be young,' Beauty replied, 'but I would rather be eaten by the Beast than die of grief at losing you. You shall not leave this house without me.'

And that was her last word. Her father and brothers grieved and protested but her sisters were secretly delighted, because they had always been jealous of her.

Meanwhile, the merchant had almost forgotten the Beast's treasure chest. He found it that night, standing at the foot of his bed, but decided to say nothing about it except to Beauty. She told him that while he was away a number of young men had visited the house and that two of them seemed to have fallen in love with her sisters. She hoped he would consent to their marriage and provide them with a dowry apiece. Beauty said this, even though she knew her sisters did not love her, because she was a good-hearted girl and she could not bear to think of them unhappy.

They, for their part, could not wait to be rid of her. As the day approached when Beauty and her father must set out for the Beast's castle, the wicked girls took to rubbing their eyes with onions, so that they might seem to be crying. But Beauty's brothers wept in earnest, for they were very fond of her. Beauty did not weep, for she would not add to their grief.

She mounted before her father and once again the horse seemed to find its own way. As night was falling they came in sight of the castle, blazing with lights and yet with no one to be seen. As before, the horse went directly to its stable and the merchant led his daughter into the great hall. Here they found a table spread with great magnificence and places laid for two.

The merchant had no heart for food but Beauty sat down and tried to encourage him by her example. To herself she thought drearily: 'I suppose the Beast wants to fatten me up before he eats me.'

They finished eating and were sitting quietly, trying to converse in a normal manner, when suddenly they heard a terrible sound, a hoarse yet thunderous roaring, like the sea in a distant cave. The merchant trembled and started to bid his daughter farewell, for he was sure that this was the Beast coming to eat her. Beauty herself could not help flinching when she caught sight of him, for the Beast was truly a fearful sight, but she forced herself to be brave. When the monster asked her if she had come to the castle of her own free will, she answered him in a small voice: 'Yes.'

'You are good,' said the Beast. 'I am much obliged to you.' He turned to the merchant. 'You, sir, leave this place tomorrow and never seek to return. Farewell, Beauty.'

'Farewell, Beast,' she replied, and with that the Beast left them.

The merchant threw his arms around his daughter. 'Oh, my dear child,' he cried. 'Save yourself! Leave me to my fate!'

'No, Father,' Beauty answered him steadfastly. 'You must go and leave me to trust in heaven's goodness.'

With that they retired to bed, each convinced they would not close their eyes. But to their surprise both fell asleep as soon as their heads touched their pillows. The merchant slept dreamlessly until morning, but Beauty, in her dreams, saw a beautiful lady standing by her bed.

'I thank you for your goodness, Beauty,' she said. 'What you have done, in gladly offering your own life for your father's, shall not go unrewarded.'

In the morning Beauty told her father of her dream, hoping to comfort him a little at their parting. But still he was full of grief and her own eyes were full of tears as she watched his bowed figure riding slowly away from the castle.

When he had gone, she ran back to the great hall and gave way to her tears. But she was a brave girl and when grief and terror had worn themselves out she sat up and began to take stock of her situation. It seemed to her unlikely that the Beast meant to devour her before the evening and so she resolved to pass the time exploring the castle.

She found it very beautiful. Each suite of rooms seemed more magnificent than the last and the views from the windows showed a landscape of well-tended woods, lakes and gardens. Then she found herself staring in surprise at a door over which was written, in letters of gold, the words:

THESE ARE BEAUTY'S ROOMS.

Beauty opened it at once and found herself in a chamber which outshone all that she had seen before. But what impressed her most was the sight of the huge bookcase which took up one whole wall and the many musical instruments with which the room was filled.

18

'I could stay here for a year,' she thought, 'and never be bored. So how could all this be given to me just for one day?'

With that thought her courage revived and she began to look about her. Going to the bookcase, she saw, inside the first book she opened, the inscription:

ALL THAT YOU SEE HERE IS YOURS.
YOUR WISH IS A COMMAND.

Beauty sighed. 'Alas,' she thought to herself. 'My only wish is to see what my poor father is doing at this moment.'

Just then her eyes fell on a tall mirror by her side and to her astonishment she saw, pictured within it, the door of her old home and her father alighting from his horse. His face was wet with tears and she saw her sisters coming to meet him. But although they tried to hide it, it was not hard for Beauty to see that in their hearts they were overjoyed. Then the scene in the mirror vanished and she saw nothing but her own reflection there. But it left her still more convinced that in this place she had nothing to fear.

At midday she again found the table set for a meal and while she ate, she listened to an admirable consort of musicians, although none was visible. But in the evening, as she took her place, there came instead of music the terrible dragging roar of the Beast's approach.

He came towards her as she sat, rigid and staring. But his voice was unexpectedly gentle.

'Beauty,' said the Beast, 'may I stay with you awhile?'

'You are the master here,' Beauty answered, trembling.

'No,' he replied. 'You alone are mistress. Bid me go, if I offend you, and I will leave you at once. Do you find me very hideous?'

'I do, of course,' Beauty admitted. 'I must tell the truth. But I think you are very kind.'

'Thank you,' said the Beast. 'But I fear I am dull as well as ugly. A great, stupid Beast.'

'It is not stupid,' Beauty said, 'to know one's limitations. No fool ever did that.'

'Eat your supper, Beauty,' said the Beast. 'Try to be happy in this place. All you see is yours and I would be sad if it failed to please you.'

'You are very kind, Beast,' Beauty answered. 'Your goodness of heart makes you seem less ugly in my eyes.'

'My heart is good, yes,' the Beast said bitterly. 'But I am a monster for all that.'

'There are many with human faces more monstrous than you,' Beauty told him. 'I prefer you, looking as you do, to those whose handsome looks hide a false and wicked heart.'

'If I were clever,' the Beast said, 'I would make you a graceful compliment for that. But I am too dull. I can only thank you.'

Beauty smiled and addressed herself to her supper. She had almost lost her fear of the Beast but all at once he startled her dreadfully by saying abruptly: 'Beauty, will you be my wife?'

 She gazed at him, trembling, afraid of arousing his anger. But at last she made herself say quietly: 'No, Beast.'

For a moment the Beast looked at her mournfully, then he heaved a great sigh, like the wind roaring down the chimney.

'Then farewell, Beauty,' he said, and with that he went from the room, turning round once in the doorway for a last unhappy look at her.

Left alone, Beauty sat for some time thinking pitifully of the poor Beast. It seemed to her very sad that he should be so kind and look so fearsome.

Three months passed and Beauty lived very pleasantly in the castle. Each evening the Beast came to her at supper-time and the two of them talked comfortably of this and that, like old friends. Beauty thought that although the Beast might not be clever, he spoke with great good sense and her regard for him grew day by day. She had grown used to his appearance and now, far from dreading the sight of him, she often caught herself glancing at the clock, counting the minutes until he would be with her again. He never failed to appear on the stroke of nine.

The only thing that continued to trouble her peace of mind was his habit of asking every night, before he left her, if she would be his wife and when she refused, as she always did, his seeming so overcome with sadness. One day she could not help telling him so.

'I am sorry, Beast. I wish I could marry you,' she said. 'But I cannot deceive you. I shall never do so. But I will always be your friend. Can you not be content with that?'

'It seems I must,' the Beast replied. 'I cannot blame you. I know I am a loathsome monster, but I love you. It is enough for me that you are willing to stay here. Tell me you will never leave me!'

Beauty felt herself blushing guiltily. She had seen in the mirror that her father was very ill, pining for his lost daughter, and she longed above everything to go to him.

'I will gladly promise to remain with you for the whole of my life,' she said, 'if only I might see my father once again! It is like a knife in my heart that he is ill and I cannot go to him.'

'It is a knife in mine,' the Beast said instantly, 'to see you unhappy. But if I send you to your father, you will surely stay with him, and then your poor Beast will die of grief.'

'No, no!' Beauty cried, almost in tears. 'I care for you too much to cause your death! I promise to return to you in a week, if you will only let me go. I saw in my mirror that my sisters are married and have left home and my brothers are all away at the wars. My father is quite alone. Let me go to him for a week.'

'You shall be there when you wake tomorrow,' the Beast said. 'Only remember your promise. Take this ring. You have only to place it on the table by your bed when you wish to return. Farewell, Beauty.'

As he uttered these words, the Beast gave one of his great sighs. Beauty went to her bed, full of sadness for the grief she had caused him.

When she woke the next morning, all thought of sadness had gone. She was in her own bed, in her father's house, with the sun slanting in her window just as it always had. She lay for a little while, contentedly, then a mischievous smile touched her lips. She reached out to the little bell that stood on her bedside table. Almost at once a maidservant, new since Beauty's leaving home, appeared in the doorway, threw up her arms and shrieked. The sound brought Beauty's father hurrying from his room and the sight of his lost daughter sitting up in bed and laughing at him was almost too much for the poor man's fragile health. He hugged her to him, laughing and crying at once, and it was a long time before either of them had eyes for anything but each other.

At last Beauty said she must get up, only she did not know what to do for clothes, since she had brought none with her. 'Oh, but you have, my lady,' the maidservant said. 'There is that great travelling trunk out in the passage. All blue leather and gold studs, it is!'

The trunk was brought in and proved to be full of wonderful dresses, each one trimmed with gold lace and diamonds. Silently thanking the Beast for his thoughtfulness, Beauty chose the simplest of them to wear that day, telling the maid to set aside some of the most magnificent ones as presents to her sisters. But the instant she said so, the whole trunkful vanished as if it had never been. Beauty stared in amazement but her father began to laugh.

'It seems the Beast has his own ideas about that,' he said. 'He means you to keep the dresses for yourself.'

At once, as if in agreement, the trunk reappeared.

Beauty got dressed and in the meanwhile messages were sent to her sisters, saying that Beauty was home, but only for a week. They soon arrived, bringing their husbands with them. Neither was happy in her marriage. The eldest had wedded a man as handsome as the day, but so in love with his own beauty that he had no eyes for her. The second had married one who was clever but whose chief use for his tongue was to quarrel with everybody, beginning with his wife. Both sisters nearly fainted with jealousy when they saw Beauty, dressed like a queen and looking more radiantly beautiful than ever.

They could hardly contain themselves as they listened to Beauty's description of the Beast's palace and the delights of her life there. As soon as they could, they escaped into the garden to plot how to spoil things for her.

'Why should she be so happy,' they said, 'when we are quite miserable?'

The eldest said: 'Sister, I have an idea. What if we were to keep her here longer than a week? That Beast of hers might be so angry when she breaks her promise to him that he'll turn on her and devour her.'

27

'Sister, I think you have it,' said the other. 'We'll keep her here at all costs.'

With this in mind they began to behave quite differently to Beauty. They sought her company, praised her looks and admired her dresses. They even invited her to their houses. Beauty was touched. She wondered if perhaps they had been sorry after all when they thought her dead. When the week was over, they wept and wailed and tore their hair, pretending such distress that Beauty was at last compelled to promise she would stay another week.

She did promise, but her heart ached when she thought of the pain she would be causing her poor Beast. She found, too, that she was missing him quite badly.

On the tenth night in her father's house, Beauty dreamt that she was back in the castle. She was walking in the gardens, beside the long lake. The Beast was lying on the grass and she knew that he was dying. His eyes reproached her for her broken promise. Beauty woke suddenly and found that her face was wet with tears.

She lay for a long while, thinking of her dream. She recalled that, for all his monstrous form, the Beast's eyes were beautiful and the look of speechless suffering in them was almost more than she could bear. 'How could I be so cruel,' she asked herself, 'when he is so good to me? Is it his fault that he is ugly? He is kind and that is worth more than beauty and cleverness put together. Why shouldn't I marry him? I would be happier than my sisters are with their husbands. Even if I cannot love him, I like and respect him, and gratitude alone should make me hesitate to wound him. I could never forgive myself.'

In another moment she was tugging off her ring. No sooner had she placed it on the table by her bed than, with a deep sigh, she fell fast asleep.

She woke to find herself back in the castle. Joyfully she sprang out of bed and only then remembered that the Beast never came to her before the evening. She had no means of knowing where he spent his days. For a long time Beauty wandered about the castle restlessly. She knew that it was no use seeking him, yet still she could not settle to her music or her books. She passed some hours dressing herself in the clothes she knew he liked but soon grew tired of her own face in the mirror, and after that there seemed nothing to do but wait.

Nine o'clock struck. But no familiar sounds echoed through the castle. No Beast entered the hall. Beauty paced the floor uneasily, remembering her dream. Still he did not come and she began to be afraid that she had killed him. Panic seized her. Filled with dread for his sake, she ran wildly through the palace, calling his name. But the fine rooms remained empty and silent. At last, near to despair, she made her way out into the darkening gardens.

Straight for the lake she ran, to the place where she had seen him in her dream. And there he lay, close by the water, just as she had feared she would find him.

With a cry of grief and remorse, Beauty cast herself down upon his body. Sure that he was dead, she clasped him in her arms, oblivious to his monstrous features. But even as she lay there weeping, she felt his heart beat faintly and, in sudden hope, she took out her handkerchief. Dipping water from the lake, she touched it to his dry lips.

Wearily the Beast opened his eyes. 'Beauty, is it you? I thought you would not come,' he whispered. 'You broke your promise and I wanted to die. But I shall die happy now that I can see you again.'

'No, no, you shall not die!' Beauty cried fiercely. 'You must live and I will marry you! I will! I believed that what I felt for you was no more than friendship but when I saw you there and thought that you were dead, I knew I could never live without you.'

No sooner had she spoken than lights sprang up all over the castle. Music and fireworks filled the night. But Beauty had no eyes for anything but the beloved Beast. Yet even as she looked at him, she saw that he was changing. The air about him shimmered, the beastly carcass blurred and fell away and he rose to stand before her, a handsome prince, fairer than the day.

'The Beast?' Beauty stammered. 'Where is he?'

'Here, at your feet,' the prince said, kneeling. 'A wicked fairy condemned me to that likeness until a lovely maiden should consent to be my bride. She made me ugly and stupid and you alone were good enough to love me for my heart alone. Now I am free to offer you the man I truly am, and not only my love but my crown.'

Gladly Beauty gave him her hand. They walked together to the castle and there, in the hall, she found her whole family assembled, transported there by the lady she had seen in her dream, who was the prince's fairy godmother.

'Welcome, Beauty,' said the fairy. 'The choice you have made in the wisdom of your heart will bring you happiness as long as you live, and you shall find beauty, wit and

kindness united in your future husband. You will become a great queen and I know that power will not mar your goodness. But for you—' Here the fairy turned to Beauty's two sisters. 'I know too well what mischief is in your hearts. To prevent it I shall clothe your bodies in stone, though your minds shall remain unchanged. Stand as two statues at your sister's gates and be it your punishment to watch the daily happiness of her life, until such time as you may truly repent. Not,' she added sadly, 'that I have much hope of repentance. Pride, anger, greed and most other deadly sins may be overcome, but for a really wicked and jealous heart there is no cure in this world.'

Thereupon the fairy waved her wand and all those present were instantly transported to the prince's kingdom, where his subjects greeted him with all imaginable joy. Beauty and the prince were married in great state and lived together throughout the length of their lives in the most perfect and deserved happiness.

POSTSCRIPT

Beauty and the Beast, now firmly established among the handful of favorite European fairytales, is in fact one of the latest comers to the children's canon. The version by Mme. Leprince de Beaumont, from which the story in this book is taken, did not appear in print until 1756. Its first English translation was in *The Young Misses Magazine* in 1761.

The theme of the beastly marriage, in which a young woman — or even a young man — is wedded to a repulsive beast or monster, goes back at least as far as classical times and occurs in all parts of the world. There are marked similarities in the tale of Cupid and Psyche, as told by Apuleius in *The Golden Ass* (second century A.D.), which he, in turn, seems likely to have obtained from an even earlier Greek source. So many of the details in the stories are the same — the palace, the nasty sisters, the return home — that, although in Psyche's case the threatened monster bridegroom turns out to be merely invisible, it is hard not to imagine a direct line of descent. But whereas Psyche's glimpse of her real bridegroom is only the start of her pilgrimage towards true intellectual or spiritual love, for Beauty the challenge is to move from the superficial to the real, to see through the loathsome outward appearance to the goodness within. Only then, when Beauty knows and loves the virtue of her Beast, can the transformation take place.

In Apuleius, as in the related stories which appear in Straparola's *Piacevoli Notti* (1550) and in Giambattista Basile's *Pentamerone* (1634), the tale, with all its symbolic implications, is intended for adults. So it was still in the version from which Mme. de Beaumont almost certainly took her story, an inordinately long-winded, 362-page narrative published in *Les Contes Marins* in 1740 by Mme. Gabrielle Susanne Barbot de Gallon de Villeneuve.

Marie Leprince de Beaumont (1711-1780) was a professional governess and the author of more than seventy books for children. She came to England in about 1745 and stayed for seventeen years, and it was in London that she published the *Magasin des enfans*, subtitled in French: 'dialogues between a good governess and some of her pupils', in which 'Beauty and the Beast' first appeared. Her interest in the story was a moral one. She belonged to a generation which believed firmly in the need for children to be instructed and edified, even in entertainment, although hers was perhaps also the first generation which considered the possibility of entertainment aimed specifically at children.

In her hands the story became the one we know today, on which all subsequent versions have been based. She loses no opportunity to drive home her points: Beauty is accomplished and industrious, as well as beautiful; the poor Beast has been cursed with stupidity as well as ugliness, or so he says. In fact, this seems to consist mainly in an inability to indulge in witty conversation. But clearly Beauty is to love him for his heart and not his mind. Virtue, by the eighteenth century, had become something quite apart from intellectual distinction.

Yet through all this, and even through Mme. de Beaumont's colloquial, unexcited prose, the old magic of the story is still strong. The compelling theme which has inspired artists of all kinds (as well as one of the most remarkable films ever made, Cocteau's *La Belle et La Bête*) is not one of moral edification. It is profound in its psychological significance, primal in its use of symbol. What we are reading about in *Beauty and the Beast* is ourselves: our strengths, our weaknesses, our painful progress towards self-knowledge and, at last, redemption.

Anne Carter

NEWMARKET PUBLIC LIBRARY